Br

06/19

Magic
Animal
Rescue

Maggie and the Unicorn

Also by E. D. Baker

The Tales of the Frog Princess:
The Frog Princess, Dragon's Breath,
Once Upon a Curse, No Place for Magic,
The Salamander Spell, The Dragon Princess,
Dragon Kiss, A Prince among Frogs,
The Frog Princess Returns

Fairy Wings
Fairy Lies

Tales of the Wide-Awake Princess:
The Wide-Awake Princess, Unlocking the Spell,
The Bravest Princess, Princess in Disguise,
Princess between Worlds, The Princess and the Pearl

A Question of Magic

The Fairy-Tale Matchmaker:
The Fairy-Tale Matchmaker,
The Perfect Match, The Truest Heart

Magic Animal Rescue:
Maggie and the Flying Horse
Maggie and the Wish Fish
Maggie and the Flying Pigs

Magic
Animal
Rescue

Maggie and the Unicorn

E. D. Baker

illustrated by
Lisa Manuzak

BLOOMSBURY
NEW YORK LONDON OXFORD NEW DELHI SYDNEY

First published in the United States of America in October 2017
by Bloomsbury Children's Books
www.bloomsbury.com

Bloomsbury is a registered trademark of Bloomsbury Publishing Plc

For information about permission to reproduce selections from this book,
write to Permissions, Bloomsbury Children's Books,
1385 Broadway, New York, New York 10018
Bloomsbury books may be purchased for business or promotional use. For
information on bulk purchases please contact Macmillan Corporate and
Premium Sales Department at specialmarkets@macmillan.com

Library of Congress Cataloging-in-Publication Data
available upon request
ISBN 978-1-68119-488-2 (paperback) • ISBN 978-1-68119-145-4 (hardcover)
ISBN 978-1-68119-146-1 (e-book)

Book design by Jeanette Levy and Colleen Andrews
Typeset by Westchester Publishing Services
Printed and bound in the U.S.A.
by Berryville Graphics Inc., Berryville, Virginia
2 4 6 8 10 9 7 5 3 1 (paperback)
2 4 6 8 10 9 7 5 3 1 (hardcover)

All papers used by Bloomsbury Publishing, Inc., are natural, recyclable
products made from wood grown in well-managed forests. The
manufacturing processes conform to the environmental regulations of the
country of origin.

*This book is dedicated to all the
fans of unicorns, and to Kim,
who first introduced me to Bob.*

Magic
Animal
Rescue

Maggie and the Unicorn

Chapter 1

"Maggie, I need help!" Bob called from just outside the stable. "We have a new patient!"

After Maggie's stepmother had kicked her out the week before, Maggie had moved in with Bob and his wife, Nora. Bob had been teaching Maggie how to care for the sick and injured animals he brought to the stable. She loved the work and was always eager to learn more.

Tucking her journal in her pocket, Maggie hurried out the door. Bob was waiting outside holding an unhappy-looking winged horse by a rope halter. The horse's head drooped, and so did her cream-colored wings.

"She's beautiful!" Maggie exclaimed. "But what's wrong with her?"

The flying horse raised her head to look at Maggie. A nasty gash was still bleeding in the middle of the animal's forehead. "She hit her head, and her depth perception is off," said Bob. "She can't judge distances very well. After I treat her wound, I'm going to put her in a stall so I can keep an eye on her. Could you please get a stall ready?"

Maggie nodded and hurried to the well for water. After filling the buckets in the stall, she spread fresh straw on the floor. Bob was struggling to clean the horse's wound when Maggie joined him.

"I could hold the halter for you if it would help," said Maggie.

"This is a wild animal," Bob told her. "I don't want you to get hurt."

Maggie stayed back while Bob gently patted the wound with a wet cloth. When the horse jerked her head away, Maggie took a step forward. Moving slowly, she reached up and stroked the horse's neck, murmuring, "Beautiful girl, we just want to help you."

The horse nudged Maggie's hand and wuffled into her hair.

"I guess she likes you," said Bob.

Maggie stroked the horse's neck while Bob cleaned the wound. The horse tried to pull away when Bob started to spread a sticky salve, but Maggie held on and continued to reassure her. When Bob was finished, he let Maggie lead the horse into the stall she'd prepared. The horse was about to bump her head on the doorframe until Maggie steered her through the opening.

"I must admit, you have a real way with the animals," Bob said as he removed the horse's halter.

Maggie shrugged. "I just try to

treat them the way I'd want to be treated if I was hurt and scared."

"Well, whatever you're doing, keep it up!" said Bob.

Maggie was closing the door when her friend Stella walked into the stable with her goose, Eglantine.

"Hi!" said Maggie. "You're awfully early." Although Stella stopped by the stable nearly every day, she usually didn't come until after lunch.

"I was hoping I could help you feed the tiny horses," Stella replied. "You haven't fed them already, have you?"

"I was just about to start," Maggie said. "I got up extra early to pick raspberries for them."

"So did I!" said Stella, holding up a small basket filled with berries. "Eglantine chased bugs while I picked these."

Leonard, the talking horse, stuck his head over his door. Dribbling grain from his mouth, he

said, "Hey, Stella! Bring any carrots for me today?"

"Of course!" she said, and held out a carrot so he could take a bite.

Eglantine hurried over to gobble up the grain that Leonard had dropped. When the goose had cleaned it all up, Maggie spread some on the floor of an empty stall. "Eglantine can stay in here while we feed the tiny horses."

Stella laughed. "All she's done this morning is eat! If she eats much more, she'll be too fat to walk."

"There's nothing wrong with that!" said Leonard.

Maggie opened the door to the tiny horses' stall. The horses were smaller than bumblebees; some had wings like butterflies, while others had wings like flies or beetles or dragonflies folded across their backs. As the girls walked in, the horses galloped to the far side of their puddle-sized lake. The moment Maggie and Stella set berries on the floor, Tickles, one of the bravest of the horses, trotted back. He came within inches of Maggie and didn't budge when she set another berry in front of him.

"He's not afraid of you anymore," Bob said from the doorway.

"Do you think he's forgiven me for accidentally breaking his wing?" Maggie asked.

"I'm sure of it!" said Bob. "He'll forgive anything as long as you keep bringing him berries!"

Chapter 2

The girls were still in the stall, playing with the tiny horses, when Nora came by carrying a covered basket. "I saw that Stella was here, so I packed you girls a picnic lunch," said Nora. "Why don't you take a break, Maggie? I know you've been up since dawn. I'm sure Bob can spare you for a little while, can't you, dear?"

"I suppose I can if I have to," he replied, but he was smiling when Maggie glanced his way.

"If you follow the stream behind the stable, you'll find a pretty little waterfall just inside the woods," said Nora. "Bob and I used to take our daughter there for picnics when she was young."

"I love waterfalls!" exclaimed Stella. "So does Eglantine!"

Maggie laughed. "Then I guess we'll have to go!"

Maggie had never had a friend like Stella before. They got along so easily, and Maggie didn't need to worry that Stella might criticize her or tattle to get her in trouble. True, Maggie had fun when she was with Bob and Nora and the animals, but she had a different kind of fun when she was with Stella. They enjoyed a lot of the same things and always had plenty to talk about. It helped that both of them were eager to try new things, too. A trip to a waterfall that would have been pleasant on her own sounded like a lot more fun with Stella.

As they followed the stream, the two girls chatted about the tiny horses. Maggie was still careful to keep an eye on what was going on around them, since the Enchanted Forest was full of dangerous creatures, while Stella watched over Eglantine.

The goose was tied to a long, pink ribbon with the other end

wrapped around Stella's wrist.
The ribbon gave the goose enough
room to hunt for bugs on the faint
path that ran beside the stream.
She was chasing a butterfly down
the path when the girls heard the
waterfall. After that, it was a race
to see who could get there first.
Eglantine was the winner.

It was a pretty spot, with the
waterfall, only a few feet high,
tumbling into a pool edged with
delicate blue flowers. The girls
found a large, flat, sun-warmed

17

rock just past the reach of the mist. Eglantine plopped into the water while the girls sat down on the rock and opened the basket.

Although Maggie hadn't felt hungry before, that changed as soon as she saw the food. Warm, crusty bread, savory sausage, and crumbling white cheese were extra delicious at the edge of a waterfall after their walk. The jug of fresh, creamy milk only made it better.

Once Eglantine saw that they were eating, she came over to beg

for bread crusts. Stella tossed her
one now and then, so they finished
the bread before anything else. The
girls were starting on the apples

they'd found in the bottom of the basket when Maggie smelled something awful. She and Stella looked up at the same time. Three goblins were arguing as they approached the other side of the pool.

"I so thirsty, I could drink all water in world!" declared one goblin.

"That not fair! I thirsty too!" cried another. "You gotta share!"

"I don't gotta do nothin'!" the first goblin shouted. "Hey, stop drinkin' my water, Geebo!"

While the two goblins argued,

the third had knelt
beside the pool
and started
lapping the
water like
a dog.

"Are those goblins?"
Stella whispered to Maggie.

"Shh!" Maggie told her friend.

It was too late. The goblins had heard them. All three heads turned their way.

Eglantine honked, eyeing the girls' apples.

"Look! Food!" declared one of the goblins.

"They don't mean our apples, do they?" Stella whispered to Maggie again.

The three goblins had already started to run around the pool. There was no way two girls and a goose could outrun them.

"No, they don't," said Maggie. "Stay where you are. I can handle this."

Maggie stood and reached into her pocket. She pulled out a small triangle that glittered in the sunlight. The goblins were only yards away when she held the triangle over her head. All three goblins stumbled to a stop.

"Unicorn!" they screeched and turned to run the other way.

"That was amazing!" Stella said, her eyes wide.

"I know," Maggie said as she sat down again and smiled. "And it works every time."

Chapter 3

Stella kept her gaze fixed on the spot where the goblins had run into the forest. Their shrieking was still loud enough to hear, even though they were a long way off. When Stella finally turned back to

Maggie, she said, "Do you think they'll come back?"

"Not anytime soon," Maggie told her.

"I've never seen goblins before," said Stella. "They smell awful, don't they?"

Maggie nodded. "Sometimes that's the first thing you'll notice about them. My father told me that if you ever smell them, but don't see them yet, run the other way."

"Does your father know a lot

about creatures like goblins?" Stella asked her.

Maggie nodded. "He has to. He works in the Enchanted Forest."

There was a sharp *crack!* as a branch broke in the forest. Birds shot from the trees to the sound of nasty laughter.

"Is that another horrible creature coming this way?" Stella asked, her face turning pale.

"Yes, but not the kind you think," said Maggie. "I'd recognize that laugh anywhere. It's my step-brother Peter. Listen, you'd better take Eglantine and hide until he's gone. He'll try to steal her from you if he has the chance."

Eglantine was one of those wonderful geese that could lay golden eggs. Maggie knew that her stepmother, Zelia, and Zelia's son Peter would do anything to get her for themselves.

While Stella picked up Eglantine and hurried into the forest,

Maggie put everything in the picnic basket so that it looked as if she'd been eating by herself. Just as she picked up the apple she'd dropped, Peter came out of trees, swinging a long stick.

"Well, if it isn't Little Miss Maggie!" he declared, wearing a familiar smirk. "Still mooching off the old man and his wife, I hear. And look at you now—stealing food and hiding in the woods so you can eat it all yourself!"

"I've never mooched off anyone," Maggie replied. She immediately wished she hadn't said anything when Peter's eyes lit up. She had learned shortly after his mother married her father that responding

to his taunts only made him keep going.

"That's not true, and you know it," said Peter. "You were mooching the entire time you lived with us! We worked day and night to give you the best food and most comfortable bed, while you daydreamed and did nothing to help us. We are so much happier with you gone. Now we all have plenty to eat and we're not nearly so cramped in the cottage. The day you left was a great day for everyone! Too bad the old man has to suffer now. But I'm sure he'll come around and realize his mistake soon enough. Then he'll kick you out and you'll have to find someone else to mooch off."

Maggie clenched her teeth so she wouldn't say anything. She worked hard now and had worked just as hard when she lived with her father's new wife and all her children. Even so, Zelia had often sent her to bed without supper. Zelia had even made Maggie give Peter the bed that her father had built for her when she was little. Everything Peter said was a lie, but it still made Maggie mad to hear it.

"Why are you here?" Maggie

asked as she picked up the picnic basket. "This is a long way from the cottage. Did you lose your sheep again?"

Peter's face turned red and he opened his mouth only to shut it. Maggie was sure he had come to spy on her, but he wasn't about to tell her that. Instead of saying anything, he walked off, whacking the stick at whatever he could reach. Maggie was careful to stay out of his way.

Waiting until long after she was

sure that Peter was gone, she finally called, "Stella, you can come out now."

A moment later, her friend emerged from the underbrush, carrying Eglantine. "I heard what he said to you," Stella told her. "He's such a horrible boy!"

"I know," Maggie replied. "If only I had something useful to scare him off with, the way I can scare off goblins!"

Chapter 4

Maggie got up early the next morning to pick more raspberries for the tiny horses. Yesterday she'd seen a berry patch on the way to the waterfall, and she thought she'd go there for a change. The berries were ripe and juicy, and in minutes her basket was almost full.

She had just popped a berry into her mouth when she saw a green-skinned girl with water lilies tucked in her long green hair stepping out of the woods. Maggie knew right away that the girl was a water nymph.

"You're the girl who visited my waterfall yesterday, aren't you?" said the nymph. "You're the one who chased off the goblins with something you held in your hand."

"Yes," Maggie said slowly.

"What was that? I ask only because I need something to chase the goblins off, too," the nymph continued.

"It was the tip of a unicorn's horn," Maggie told her. "Goblins are afraid of unicorns because they can get rid of poison. There's a lot of poison in goblins."

"I didn't know that," said the nymph. "I have to ask, do you have an extra piece of unicorn horn that I could use? I'd be happy to give you something in exchange."

"I don't have any extras," Maggie confessed. "But even if I did, you wouldn't have to pay me for it."

"Oh," the nymph said, looking distressed. "I was so hoping you had *something* you could give me. Those goblins come by every day, and I have to hide underwater until they leave. I really wish I had a way to scare them off like you did."

Maggie dropped one last berry

in her basket before saying, "I'll see what I can do. The tips of unicorn horns grow back after they break off. There's always a chance I'll find another."

Hurrying back to the stable, Maggie began looking for Bob. She found him in the kitchen with Nora, finishing a last cup of tea before starting his morning chores.

"I saw a water nymph in the woods today," Maggie said as she set the basket filled with berries on the kitchen table. "She wanted to know if we had any more pieces of unicorn horns. She's afraid of the goblins and they keep going back to her pool under the waterfall."

"I'm sorry," Bob said, shaking his head. "I don't have any to spare."

"Would you mind if I looked in the unicorn's stall? Maybe there's one in the straw on the floor."

"Go right ahead," said Bob. "You might want to tie Randal in the aisle of the stable while you look, though. He can be very grumpy."

"Thanks!" Maggie said and gave

him a kiss on the cheek. As she turned to go back to the stable, she caught a glimpse of the look Bob gave Nora. It was a pleased smile that made Maggie smile too.

Randal was the only unicorn living in the stable at the moment. Years before, Bob had found him caught in a hunter's trap, with his leg too badly injured to save. Bob had made him a peg leg, which helped the unicorn get around but gave him a very odd gait. When Maggie led Randal out of his stall, the clop, clop, *thump!*, clop made Leonard stick his head over his own stall door.

"What are you doing?" he asked. "You should be feeding me, not fooling around with old Twinkle Toes."

"I'll get your food in a minute," Maggie told him as she tied the unicorn's lead line to a hook on the wall. "I'm just looking for something."

Leonard watched as Maggie returned to the stall with a pitchfork to sift through the straw. "Hey, if you're looking for something, I've got plenty for you to find in my stall!"

Maggie laughed. "I'll clean your stall later. I'm trying to see if there are any broken-off tips of Randal's horn in the straw. I met a water nymph who could really use one. What's this?" she asked, picking up something hard and curved. "Do you think the trimmings from unicorn hooves might work to scare off goblins?"

Leonard's head disappeared from above the stall as he returned to check his still-empty feed pan. "If I say 'yes,' will you feed me now?"

"Never mind," she said, tucking it in her pocket. "I'll ask Bob."

"I have no idea," Bob said when he came to the stall a few minutes later. "I suppose it's worth a try."

"Then I'll go see the nymph right after I finish feeding everyone and cleaning their stalls. She seemed pretty desperate."

"Aren't we all?" said Leonard. "Where *is* my breakfast?"

Maggie hurried through her chores. She was cleaning her last stall when Bob stuck his head in and said, "Here, you can give the nymph this, too. I trimmed Randal's mane. Now the water nymph can test a few things."

"Thanks!" Maggie told him, taking the hair clippings from his hand. "If one thing doesn't work, maybe another one will."

The nymph wasn't near the berry patch when Maggie went back. She wasn't sitting by the water-fall, either. However, when Maggie called, "Miss Water Nymph, I have something for you to try!" a head appeared in the middle of the pool.

"My name is Lily," the nymph said as she waded out of the water. "Did you find an extra piece of horn?"

"No, but I did bring some other things you can try. Here's a piece of a unicorn's hoof and some clip-pings from his mane. I have no idea if either one will work. Don't depend on them to scare off the goblins for good until you've had a chance to test them."

Lily smiled as she took the items from Maggie. "Thank you so much!

I'll put these out where the goblins can't miss them and see what happens. What can I give you in exchange?"

"Like I already said, you don't owe me anything," said Maggie.

"Pish posh!" the nymph replied. "I always pay my debts. Just let me know if I can ever help you. This means a lot to me!"

Chapter 5

A few days later, Maggie and Nora were sitting in the kitchen mending clothes when Bob came back from a trip to the village looking worried. "What's wrong?" Nora asked as she helped him out of his jacket.

"I heard a rumor that there's an injured unicorn in the forest," Bob said. "I need a maiden to help me catch it. I asked around in the village, but the last one got married a few months ago. I don't know what I'm going to do now."

"I can help!" said Maggie.

Bob shook his head. "You're much too young, Maggie. We're talking about a wild

animal that can be very dangerous whether or not it's in pain. I
don't want you to get hurt."

"But I helped you with the flying
horse the other day," said Maggie.
"She was good for me, and you
said *she* was a wild animal."

"That's true," said Bob, "but this
is different. Flying horses aren't
nearly as spirited as unicorns. My
mind is made up. I don't want you
anywhere near that unicorn until
I'm convinced it isn't going to hurt
you."

"I've already touched a wild unicorn, remember? The silver unicorn put his head in my lap the first day I saw him. And he helped me in the rainstorm after Zelia kicked me out. The only time I've seen him act spirited was when the goblins came after me and he chased them off. He's helped me twice now, and I don't think he would ever hurt me."

"You're probably right about that," said Bob.

"If you let me help you, I'll do

exactly what you say. You can teach me everything I'll need to know before we go anywhere near the unicorn."

"I'm not sure about this," Bob said, rubbing his chin.

"Please?" Maggie asked, crossing her fingers behind her.

Although she'd known that Peter had been lying earlier, the things he'd said still bothered her. If she could truly help Bob in some significant way, she'd know that she was earning her keep.

Bob sighed and glanced at Nora. His wife nodded and flicked her gaze at Maggie. "Oh, all right," said Bob. "The animals seem to really like you, including the wild ones. But you have to do precisely what I tell you!"

Maggie's eyes lit up. "Oh, I will! I promise!"

"Then the first thing you have to remember is to stay calm. No sudden movements and no loud noises," said Bob.

"I can do that," Maggie told him.

"You'll sit where I tell you to and stay perfectly still. You may have to wait a while before the unicorn shows up," said Bob.

"All right," Maggie replied.

"When it does, don't move while it settles down beside you. Stroke its head until it closes its eyes. You can put the lead line on it then. Just a minute. I'll show you how it works."

Bob got to his feet and strode into his bedroom. When he came back out, he held a blue and silver braided rope. "Slip it around the unicorn's neck like this, then make a knot like this. Here, practice and show me that you can do it."

Maggie took the line and practiced until she didn't have to think about how to make the knot and could do it without looking.

"It's a special line that I had made just for catching unicorns," said

Bob. "They are very vain animals, and this lead is extra pretty. The unicorn shouldn't mind once it sees what you put on it. When the lead line is on, you'll stand up and walk the unicorn all the way to the stable. No one else can touch the unicorn until you put it in its stall."

"I understand," said Maggie. "When are we going to do this?"

"As soon as we've fed all the animals," said Bob. "Leonard will never forgive us if we don't feed him before we leave!"

Chapter 6

Maggie and Bob walked through the forest, making as little noise as possible. The man who had told Bob about spotting an injured unicorn had given him good directions, but Maggie hadn't realized they were going near her old home until they were almost there. When they reached a familiar meadow near the pond where Peter liked to fish, Bob stopped and pointed at a spot on the ground.

"Sit right here," he said. "Here's the lead line. Remember, don't make a sound."

Maggie nodded as she took the rope and sat down. After hiding the lead line under her, she made herself comfortable and settled back to wait. She watched the swallows, soaring and swooping as they snagged insects from the air. She watched the grasshoppers leaping from one blade of coarse grass to another. After she'd been sitting still for a while, she spotted fairies flitting between the wildflowers. She looked up when a hawk flew overhead, screeching. When she looked down again, a palomino unicorn was watching her from the edge of the meadow. Even from that far, she could see the gash in his side and the gouges on his leg. The unicorn must have fought with something big and nasty to have injuries like those.

Maggie scarcely breathed as the unicorn limped toward her. She didn't move as he snuffled her hair with his lips, or as he lay down beside her and rested his head in her lap. He gazed up at her as she raised her hand ever so slowly. Moments after Maggie began to stroke his head, the unicorn closed his eyes.

Maggie smoothed the unicorn's

forelock and caressed his head until the animal's heartbeat slowed and she thought he might be asleep. Carefully, she drew the lead line out from under her and fastened it around the unicorn's neck.

Maggie knew that some people tried to catch unicorns so they could steal their magical horns. She would never help someone like that, but it made her feel good to help Bob, who only wanted to take care of the animals. After petting the unicorn one last time, she gently lifted his heavy head off her lap. "It's time to go," she whispered and got to her feet.

The unicorn jumped up and shook himself. Stopping suddenly, he turned his head to look at his side, as if he had just remembered that he was injured.

Maggie held tightly to the lead line as she began to walk out of the meadow. Bob had stayed to watch over her, and she noticed him now, leading the way through the trees. The unicorn followed her as docilcly as an old plow horse, his head bumping into her arm as they walked.

They had just reached the well-trodden path that led to her family's cottage when Maggie saw her stepbrother Peter poking a stick at something on the ground. By the time she reached him, Bob was already there, looking angry. Peter had come across a large bird that seemed to be in bad shape. Maggie wasn't sure, but she thought it might be a phoenix at the end of its unusual life. She was just walking up when the bird cried out and suddenly burst into flames. With a shout, Peter grabbed a bucket from the ground beside him and tossed the water on the burning bird.

"No! Don't!" yelled Bob as the

fire fizzled and went out. The bird squawked and fell over to lie in the ash-filled puddle.

The shouts and the splashing water had startled the unicorn. He reared, striking the air with his front hooves. Maggie backed away, still holding the lead line. "You're all right," she said in a calming voice. "No one is going to hurt you."

The unicorn screamed once before settling back on all four legs. His nostrils flared as he snorted and pawed the ground. As soon as she had the unicorn calmed, Maggie turned back to Bob and Peter.

"Why did you do that?" Bob asked Maggie's stepbrother.

"What, save its life?" said Peter. "The stupid bird was on fire!"

"It's a phoenix," said Bob. "It bursts into flame when it's old and about to die and is reborn in its own ashes! Dumping water on it will put out the fire and leave the bird alive, but in terrible pain."

"How was I supposed to know that?" demanded Peter.

"I didn't think you would," said Bob. "What I want to know is why you were poking it with a stick."

"It came after me," said Peter. "I was taking a bucket of water to my mother when that bird attacked me out of nowhere."

"I doubt that very much," said Bob. "Phoenixes are actually very shy birds and never attack anyone. You'll have to come up with a better story than that!"

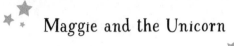

"I don't have to explain myself to you!" shouted Peter. He turned as if he'd just noticed Maggie and the unicorn. "What do you have there, Mags?"

Maggie stepped in front of the unicorn as Peter walked up, swinging the empty bucket. She glanced at Bob, who was studying the phoenix as he took off his jacket. Carefully wrapping the jacket around the bird, he scooped it into his arms.

Maggie stumbled to the side when the unicorn bumped her. Sticking his head into Peter's face, the unicorn opened his mouth and screamed so loudly that it made

Maggie's ears hurt. She clapped her hands over her ears and waited to see what Peter would do. The bucket clattered as it fell to the ground. A moment later, Peter disappeared among the trees.

"Thank you for that," Maggie told the unicorn and reached up to pat his neck. The animal bumped her with his head and nickered. It looked as if Maggie had made another friend.

Chapter 7

After getting the unicorn and the
phoenix back to the stable, Maggie
and Bob spent the rest of the day
caring for them. Bob washed the
gashes in the unicorn's side and
legs while Maggie stood by the

animal's head, whispering calming words. "Bob is trying to help you, beautiful boy. We'll have you all better in no time!"

"Here, hold these," Bob said, handing her bandages. Smearing a salve on the wounds, he took the bandages back and used them to wrap the unicorn's leg.

"Do you have any idea what could have hurt him like that?" Maggie asked Bob.

"It was probably a troll," said

Bob. "They can do a lot of damage with their claws, which are sharp and filthy enough to cause a bad infection. I just hope we got to him in time. The salve should help, but it may not be enough."

After making sure that the unicorn had everything he needed, Maggie and Bob turned their attention to the phoenix. The bird lay shivering on the floor of the stall where Bob had placed it. Most of its feathers had burned away.

Maggie thought it looked like a singed, plucked chicken. When she knelt down beside the phoenix, it didn't even raise its head to look at her.

"The phoenix will be fine, won't it?" asked Maggie.

"I don't know," said Bob. "I've never seen something like this before. All I know is, that bird has to get stronger than it is now before it can transform in the fire."

Maggie frowned and turned back to the bird. "What do we need to do to help it?"

"Make it as comfortable as we can and hope for the best," Bob replied. "I have another salve that will ease the pain, but I don't know if it will be enough to save a phoenix in this condition."

The phoenix made weak little sounds as Bob coated it in the salve and poured a thick liquid down the bird's throat. "I'd like to stay here for a while, if you don't mind," said Maggie.

"That's a good idea," Bob replied. "Let me know if either of our patients takes a turn for the worse."

Bob was on his way out the door when Maggie sat down beside the phoenix. Taking her journal out of her pocket, she opened to one of the pages she'd already started.

Unicorns:

Appearance—Most look like slender, delicate horses. Don't let this fool you! They are very strong and fast.

Horn—Spiral, shining, usually beautiful. Can be as long as a grown man's arm. One touch of the horn can get rid of poison. Note: Pieces of a unicorn's horn can scare off goblins.

Mane and tail—long and thick. Very beautiful.

Temperament—Nice around friends. Angry

and fierce around goblins and
other enemies.

After checking the point on her
pencil, Maggie added:

Weapons—
They can use their horns for
poking or whacking.

She thought a moment before
writing:

They can scream very loudly and
scare people away.

To catch a unicorn—A girl must
sit in the forest or meadow
without moving or making a

sound until the unicorn approaches her. She must hold perfectly still while the unicorn sniffs her and lies down beside her. Once the unicorn's head is in her lap, she may pet the unicorn. After the unicorn closes its eyes, the girl can fasten a lead line around its neck. The girl may then lead the creature out of the forest.

Note: Avoid nasty boys and flaming phoenixes while leading a unicorn!

After rereading what she had written, Maggie turned to a clean page and continued writing.

Phoenix:

Appearance—
As big as a
buzzard, only pretty.
Bright red,
yellow, and
orange feathers.

Unusual habits—When a
phoenix gets old, its feathers
start looking shabby. It will
burst into flames and rise from the
ashes young and beautiful again.
Dousing the flames will stop the
process and the bird will be in a lot
of pain. If that happens, cover him
with a salve to make him more
comfortable. Then
wait and hope
that he gets
better.

Chapter 8

Maggie stayed with the injured animals until Bob came out for the evening feeding. When they had finished, he turned to Maggie. "You need to come in now," he said. "Nora is making a special supper for us. She knows how hard you've been working."

"I'd like to stay out here to watch over the phoenix and the unicorn a little while longer, if you don't mind," said Maggie. "They're both hurting and—"

Bob shook his head. "Neither one will notice if you leave now. Come inside, Maggie. Your supper will get cold."

"Did you tell Nora about the phoenix?" Maggie asked as she followed him from the stable.

"I did," said Bob. "I also told her how worried you are. I know you care for the animals, but you can't let yourself get too attached to them. If they don't get better, well, they won't be around much longer. And if they do get better, we'll release them into the forest. Either way, they won't be here for long."

"I know," said Maggie. "I guess it's just that I wanted to make them feel better. I hate knowing that they're suffering."

"You've already made a difference," Bob told her. "Neither one would be here if it wasn't for you.

And since they arrived, you've taken excellent care of them both."

Maggie sighed. "If only I could do more."

They went inside for a delicious supper of baked trout, fresh peas, and salad. Nora had made three-berry pie for dessert. Maggie was eating her second big piece of pie when there was a sharp knock on

the door. She started to get up to answer it, but Bob gestured for her to sit down again.

"Unexpected visitors after dark are never a good thing," he told her. "It could mean that an animal is hurt . . . or worse."

"What could be worse than an injured animal?" Maggie asked Nora as Bob went to the door.

When the door swung open, Zelia and Peter were standing outside.

"That!" Nora whispered.

Zelia shoved Peter inside before

Bob could close the door. She stepped in after him and scowled at Bob. "We've come for our share," she announced.

"Your share of what?" asked Bob. "If you mean the three-berry pie, I'm afraid we've eaten most of it."

"I'm talking about the money you'll get for selling the unicorn!" said Zelia. "Peter tells me that Maggie helped you catch one today. Everyone knows that people get a lot of money for a unicorn."

Maggie jumped to her feet. "We

didn't catch that unicorn to sell it! We caught it to tend its wounds and help it get better!"

Zelia's face turned red as she took another step into the room. "You're lying again! You want to sell that unicorn and keep all that money for yourselves. We're your family and we deserve that money!"

"Maggie doesn't lie," Bob said, his voice cold. "We brought that unicorn here because it was hurt. It isn't for sale! Besides, you stopped deserving anything from

89

her the day you kicked her out of your cottage into a bad storm. Now get out and don't come back!"

"This isn't right," shouted Zelia. "You owe me that money!"

"Out!" Bob roared.

"You haven't heard the last of this!" Zelia cried even as she backed away.

"Oh, yes I have!" Bob said, slamming the door behind Zelia and Peter. He came to sit at the table again, and turned to Maggie. "I am going to pay you for what you did today, but I wasn't going to tell Zelia that."

"You don't have to pay me for anything!" said Maggie. "I would do any work you ask of me without being paid. You've given me a home and a family, which is more than enough. I'm just sorry that Zelia showed up again like that. She has no right to bother you."

"The only thing that bothers me is that she won't leave you alone," said Bob. "That woman shouldn't even be talking to you!"

Chapter 9

Maggie didn't sleep well that night. The things Zelia said had upset her, and it wasn't because she felt as if she owed her stepmother anything. It was because Zelia had once again barged into Bob and Nora's peaceful home and demanded something that wasn't hers. Was Zelia ever going to leave them alone?

Zelia's visit wasn't the only thing that kept Maggie awake, however. She was worried about the injured unicorn and the phoenix. Their pain-filled eyes haunted Maggie every time she tried to go to sleep.

She woke early the next morning and was dressed and on her way to the stable before anyone else was out of bed. While the unicorn looked just like it had the night before, the phoenix looked worse.

It didn't react when she sat down beside it and barely made a sound when she brushed a piece of straw off its wing. She was trying to get it to take a sip of water when Bob stepped into the stall.

"Is this a boy or a girl?" she asked him. "I don't want to keep calling this bird 'it.'"

"I don't know," Bob said. "The males and females look the same. We wouldn't know unless it laid an egg. That's something you might want to put in your journal."

"I will," said Maggie. "Look at this. I can't get it to drink."

Bob sighed and shook his head. "Then it's in worse shape than I feared. Come help me feed the others. We'll see how your patients are when we finish."

The animals were quiet that morning. Maggie was sure they knew what was going on. She worked faster than ever, hurrying Bob as he scooped the feed into buckets.

When she was finished, she

checked on the unicorn. He stood in the stall with his head hanging down. When Maggie petted him, she thought he felt hot.

Maggie checked on the phoenix next. It didn't even open its eyes.

"Anyone here?" Stella called from the doorway.

"I'm glad you came," Bob replied. "Maggie needs a break. Please go for a walk with her."

"But I don't—" Maggie began.

"Go!" said Bob. "You need fresh air and a change of scenery."

As soon as the girls left the stable, Eglantine started pulling them in the direction of the waterfall. "I guess I know where she wants to go!" said Stella. "Now, tell me what's wrong. You look worried about something."

Maggie started telling her about how she had caught the injured unicorn. They were nearing the waterfall when she reached the part of the story where Peter had poured water on the flaming

phoenix. "The bird was badly burned, but it can't complete its transformation. It's in a lot of pain now and we don't know if it's going to make it."

"I knew I didn't like that boy Peter!" Stella exclaimed.

"The unicorn is sick, too. It probably got an infection from a troll's claws. I just wish I knew how to help them," said Maggie. Having reached the pool, Eglantine scurried to the edge and plopped in.

She was chasing minnows when the nymph rose out of the water.

"Who is that?" Stella whispered to Maggie.

"Stella, I'd like you to meet Lily. Lily, this is my friend Stella," she told the nymph. "Did the pieces of the hoof or the mane trimmings help?"

"Not as well as the piece of unicorn horn, but I think they made the goblins uncomfortable enough that they didn't stay long.

Even that is an improvement. Thank you again. I know you said I didn't owe you anything, but I heard you talking. Can you take me to see the unicorn and the phoenix? I think I might be able to help them."

"It would be wonderful if you could!" Maggie cried.

"You go on ahead," Stella told her. "I'll be along as soon as I can get Eglantine out of the water."

Maggie hurried back to the stable with Lily.

"I didn't know this was so close to my waterfall!" the nymph said when she spotted the buildings. "I don't think I've ever come this way before. I rarely have a reason to go near humans."

"Bob has been helping animals here for years," said Maggie. "He and his wife, Nora, are wonderful!"

Maggie led Lily back to the stall where Bob was bending over the phoenix. The bird was barely breathing. "You're back already," he said when he saw Maggie.

"Bob, this is Lily," said Maggie. "She said that she might be able to help the phoenix and the unicorn."

Lily reached into the pouch she was carrying and took out a small clay bottle. "This is healing water that I got from a special spring," she told them. Kneeling beside the phoenix, she pulled the cork out of the little bottle. Ever so carefully, she sprinkled the water on the wings of the phoenix.

"The bird looks the same as it did, only wet!" said Maggie.

"Give it time," Lily told her.

They all looked toward the door when Stella walked in with her goose under one arm. "Sorry it took so long. I had a hard time catching Eglantine. Wow! Would you look at that!" she said, pointing at the phoenix.

Everyone turned to look. Feathers were sprouting all over the phoenix as it raised its head. It was wobbling on its feet moments later. Opening its beak, it cried out just as it had in the forest.

"Get back!" Bob shouted, dragging the girls away from the bird.

There was a flash and the phoenix was engulfed in flames. Maggie and her friends watched as the fire crackled and grew higher. When it finally died down, a young, healthy bird stood in the ashes.

Spreading its wings, the phoenix flew out of the stall, down the aisle, and out the stable door.

"Thank you so much!" Maggie said to Lily. "That was amazing!"

"I've never seen anything like it!" exclaimed Bob.

"I'm glad I got here in time to see that," Stella said as she tried to control her squirming goose. "But I think I should go now. Eglantine wants to finish our walk."

Chapter 10

"I'm glad the healing water worked so well," Lily said as Stella left the barn. "I wasn't sure what it would do, just that it should help. May I see the unicorn now?"

The unicorn was lying on his side when they walked into his stall.

Lily sat beside him and dribbled some of the healing water into his mouth. He swallowed a little, but Maggie wasn't sure it was enough to make a difference.

"He isn't drinking much," said Maggie. "Is that little bit going to help him?"

Lily shrugged. "We'll have to wait and see."

"Maggie," said Bob, "can you help me clean up after the phoenix? I have to get rid of those ashes."

"I'll be right back," Maggie told Lily and left to help Bob.

He was waiting for her with a bucket and two shovels. They were scooping up the ashes when Maggie had an idea. "What are you going to do with these?" she asked, tapping the ashes with her shovel.

"Toss them in the compost pile, I suppose," said Bob.

"May I have them?" Maggie asked him.

"Sure, but why would you want a pile of ashes?"

"The phoenix is a magical bird, right?" said Maggie. "Do you think some of the phoenix's magic might still be in the ashes? Maybe we can use them to help the unicorn."

"It's worth a try," Bob told her.

When they had all the ashes collected, Maggie took the bucket back to the stall. "Do you think a paste made from the phoenix's ashes and your healing water might help the unicorn?" she asked Lily.

"Maybe," said Lily. "What do you have in mind?"

"We can put the paste on his wounds and see if it will draw out the infection," Maggie said, sitting down beside the water nymph.

Lily stroked the unicorn's forelock. The animal's ears didn't even flicker. "I suppose it can't hurt. We might as well try it."

Maggie scooped up some of the ashes with her hand. After Lily poured a few drops of healing water on it, Maggie stirred the ashes and water together, making a gray

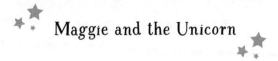
paste. The wounds on the animal's leg were hot and swollen when Maggie smeared the paste on them.

She didn't expect anything to happen right away, so she was surprised when the paste began to bubble and froth while turning a sickly yellow. The paste seemed to boil away. When it was gone, the swelling was down and the wound was no longer hot.

The girls made more paste and spread it on all of the unicorn's wounds. Once again, the paste bubbled and frothed. After a few minutes, the unicorn raised his head and looked around. His eyes looked clear and not pain-filled, the way they had before.

"It looks as if that was a really good idea, Maggie!" Bob said from the doorway.

Lily gave the unicorn more of the healing water to drink. Maggie had to jump out of the way when the unicorn scrambled to his feet, bumping his horn against the wall. She saw something glitter and fall to the floor. When she bent down, she found the tip of the unicorn's horn.

"Here," she said, handing it to Lily. "It's a gift to you from the unicorn."

Lily's eyes lit up. "I'd love to take it, but are you sure it's all right?" she said, glancing from Maggie to Bob.

"You deserve it," said Maggie. "Without your help, the unicorn and the phoenix might not have made it."

Bob nodded. "She's right. The

tip of his horn is yours. Thank you for all your help."

Lily looked at the glittering piece of horn in her hand and smiled. "So much for those goblins. Once they know I have this, they probably won't come around anymore. Thank you!" she said and gave Maggie and Bob big hugs.

"We're not the ones you should thank," said Bob.

Lily turned to the unicorn and threw her arms around his neck. "And thank you!" she cried as the unicorn wuffled her hair.

"I need to go now, but is it all right if I come back tomorrow?" she asked Bob.

"Of course!" he said. "You can come back any time you want. You were a very big help today."

When Maggie walked the water nymph to the door, Lily handed her the clay bottle. "It's still about half full," said Lily. "You keep it. I know you'll put it to good use."

Maggie waved as the nymph walked away. She turned when she realized that Bob was standing beside her. "You can't say that you don't make a difference, Maggie," he said. "The phoenix and the unicorn both got better because of you."

"Oh, no, that was because of Lily. She's the one who brought the healing water."

"And she wouldn't have come here at all if it hadn't been for you," said Bob. "You're a very special girl, and your friends know it. You were the one who thought of making that paste. That was a great idea. I'll find something to store the rest of the ashes in. You should put everything you learned today in your journal."

"Then I need to get started," said Maggie. "Because I have an awful lot to write!"

About the Author

E. D. Baker is the author of the Tales of the Frog Princess series, the Wide-Awake Princess series, the Fairy-Tale Matchmaker series, and many other delightful books for young readers, including *A Question of Magic*,

Fairy Wings, and *Fairy Lies*. Her first book, *The Frog Princess*, was the inspiration for Disney's hit movie *The Princess and the Frog*. She lives with her family and their many animals in rural Maryland.

www.talesofedbaker.com